MERMAID AND PIRATE

by TRACEY BAPTISTE

illustrated by LEISL ADAMS

Algonquin Young Readers   2023

Published by
Algonquin Young Readers
an imprint of Workman Publishing Co., Inc.
a subsidiary of Hachette Book Group, Inc.
1290 Avenue of the Americas
New York, New York 10104

Hachette Livre
58 rue Jean Bleuzen
92 178 Vanves Cedex, France

Hachette Book Group, UK
Carmelite House
50 Victoria Embankment, London EC4Y 0DZ

LIBRARY OF CONGRESS CATALOGING-IN-PUBLICATION DATA

Names: Baptiste, Tracey, author. | Adams, Leisl, illustrator.
Title: Mermaid and pirate / Tracey Baptiste ; illustrated by Leisl Adams.
Description: First edition. | Chapel Hill, North Carolina : Algonquin Young Readers, 2022. | Audience: Ages 4-8 |
Audience: Grades K-1 | Summary: "An encounter between a brown mermaid and pirate launches a humorous tale
of friendship that shows how kindness and empathy go beyond words."—Provided by publisher.
Identifiers: LCCN 2022014358 | ISBN 9781643750774 (hardcover)
Subjects: CYAC: Mermaids—Fiction. | Pirates—Fiction. | Friendship—Fiction. | Kindness—Fiction.
Classification: LCC PZ7.B229515 Mer 2022 | DDC [Fic]—dc23
LC record available at https://lccn.loc.gov/2022014358

10 9 8 7 6 5 4 3 2 1

First Edition

For Norah, William, and Eli
—T. B.

For J.T. and Jason
—L. A.

A storm was gathering on the horizon.

"GOOD," said the mermaid.

She liked storms.

She liked to roll with the waves
and dance to the beat of the rain
on the sea.

"EXCELLENT,"
said the pirate.

He loved storms.

He liked how the wind whipped
the water and snapped the ropes
and made even crossing
the deck a challenge.

The storm came and the water grew rough. The wind tore at the sails.
Barrels of food and boxes of supplies tumbled into the sea.

Lightning split the mast down the middle. The wood creaked. It groaned.

The mast snapped off the deck and fell
into the roaring sea. The mermaid swam after it.
The pirate cast a net to catch it.

It didn't work out quite the way either of them expected.

"TERRIFIC," said the pirate.
"NOW I'LL SINK!"

"GREAT," said the mermaid.
"NOW I'M STUCK."

That is not what
the mermaid and
pirate heard.

The mermaid heard, Aargh.

The pirate heard, Glub glub!

The mermaid fumed.

The pirate sighed.
He helped her out of the nets.

IT . . .

WAS . . .

NOT . . .

EASY.

The pirate dove into the deep to hide his treasure—
gold, silver, necklaces, rings! He found the perfect spot.

"THAT'S NOT A GOOD SPOT,"
said the mermaid.

The pirate pushed his treasure
under a large chunk of coral.

"WATCH OUT!" the mermaid said. Blub!

A hungry-looking shark
swam fast toward the pirate.

Rows and rows of teeth gleamed in her mouth.
The pirate reached for his dagger.
The shark opened her mouth wide
and made one big . . .

. . . TURN.

The mermaid and pirate swam to the surface.

Aaaarrrgggghhhh?

"I TOLD HER YOU WERE TOO BITTER,"
the mermaid said.

Gluuuuuuub.

Water was filling the pirate's ship.

The mermaid brought him pieces of the broken mast.

"THANK YOU," the pirate said.
"BUT THAT WON'T HELP."

"THIS WON'T HELP, WILL IT?"
the mermaid said.

Another ship sailed by.

"AHOY!" called its captain.
"DO YOU NEED HELP?"

The pirate turned. The mermaid looked up.

"**WAIT A MINUTE,**" said the captain.

"**IS THAT A . . . MERMAID?**"

"**THAT,**" said the pirate, "**IS WHAT'S LEFT OF MY BROKEN MAST.**"

The captain frowned.

The pirate smiled.

The captain threw the pirate a rope.
"HERE," he said.
"I'LL TOW YOU BACK TO LAND."

"THANK YOU!" the pirate said.

AcK.

"THANK YOU!" the mermaid said from the depths.

"I HAVE TO GO NOW," he said.

"I KNOW YOU HAVE TO GO," the mermaid said.

Every now and then, the mermaid would find
a small coin wrapped in seaweed.

Every now and then, the pirate would find
a pink shell floating on the water.

The pirate fixed his ship
and looked out across the sea.
He saw a flash in the water.

The mermaid sang her songs and studied the horizon.
She saw a familiar ship on the waves.

"HELLO, FRIEND,"
said the pirate.

"HELLO, FRIEND,"
said the mermaid.

Aargh.

Glubbity.

Ahhh. The pirate smiled.

The mermaid smiled. Lub.

Glarb,
they said together as they turned and swam toward the horizon.